NOAH NOASAURUS

NO

ELAINE KIELY KEARNS   ILLUSTRATED BY COLIN JACK

Albert Whitman & Company
Chicago, Illinois

For Tara and Meghan, who are never grumpy.
And for Bobby, who's grumpy,
but only in the morning—EKK

Library of Congress Cataloging-in-Publication data is on file with the publisher.

Text copyright © 2019 by Elaine Kiely Kearns
Illustrations copyright © 2019 by Albert Whitman & Company
Illustrations by Colin Jack
First published in the United States of America in 2019 by Albert Whitman & Company
ISBN 978-0-8075-5703-7

Printed in China
10 9 8 7 6 5 4 3 2 1 WKT 22 21 20 19 18

Design by Ellen Kokontis

For more information about Albert Whitman & Company,
visit our website at www.albertwhitman.com.

100 Years of Albert Whitman & Company
Celebrate with us in 2019!

Noah Noasaurus woke up feeling very

NO to his woolly
mammoth slippers.

NO to the taste of
Smilodon toothpaste.

NO to the smell of
scrambled dodo eggs.

"How about some Jurassic toast?" asked his mother.

"Wanna play Prehistoric People?" asked his brother.

"Good morning, Noah Noasaurus,"
said Toby Rex. "Where are you off to?"
"Nowhere," Noah grumbled.
"**NOWHERE**? Ooooooh, that sounds fun!
I'll come with you!"

Noah kept walking.

"Good day!" said Brian BrontO'Saurus. "Where are you two headed?"

"We're exploring!" blurted Toby. "Want to join?"

"S'pose I could stretch my legs," said Brian. "Count me in!"

Noah sped up.

"Hi-ho!" sang Tom Iguanodon. "What are y'all up to?"

"Getting some exercise," called Brian.

"Wonderful!" said Tom, stepping in. "I'll sing you my new tune!"

Noah plugged his ears.

"Pardon me," said Ava Ceratops. "May I ask where everyone is going?"

"For a stroll!" called Tom.

"Fabulous," said Ava. "I'd love the company." And she too squeezed into the line.

Noah was no longer listening.

Noah climbed over a jagged rock. But the other dinosaurs followed.

He crawled through a log.
But the dinosaurs followed!

He jumped over a massive puddle and...

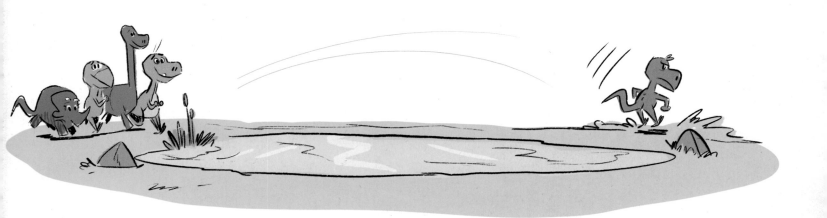

Those pesky dinosaurs had followed.

Noah's face blazed hot.

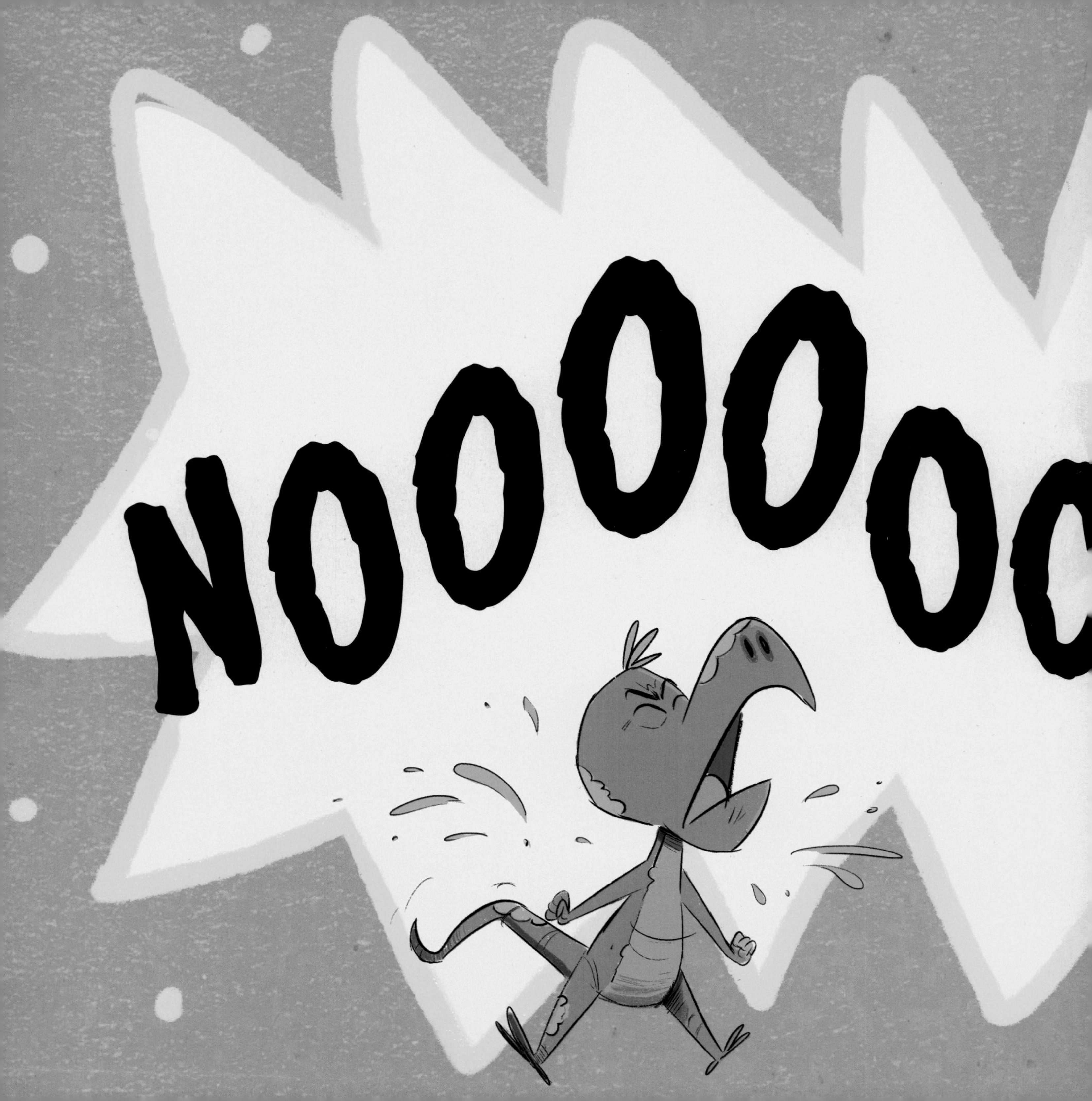
NOOOOOO

Noah stomped his feet.

LEFT.

RIGHT.

LEFT.

RIGHT.

Finally, Toby Rex spoke.
"What a **GREAT** idea, Noah! **LET'S MARCH!**"

So they all stamped their feet.

LEFT!

RIGHT!

LEFT!

RIGHT!

"LOOK!" said Trudy Trachodon. "A PARADE!"

Noah spun around to see the dinosaurs behind him. "**GRUGHHH!**" he huffed. "Fine! I'll do **NOTHING!**"

"Aren't you coming, Noah?"
called Toby Rex.

Noah looked down at his muddy self.
He looked up at his muddy friends.
Then he opened his mouth and let
out a great, big, dinosaur...

Noah stomped back into line.
"Come on everybody," he called.
"Let's march to **NOWHERE!**"

As they went, Ava Ceratops asked, "Is there anything better than a muddy parade with friends?" Noah Noasaurus flashed a wide smile and shouted...